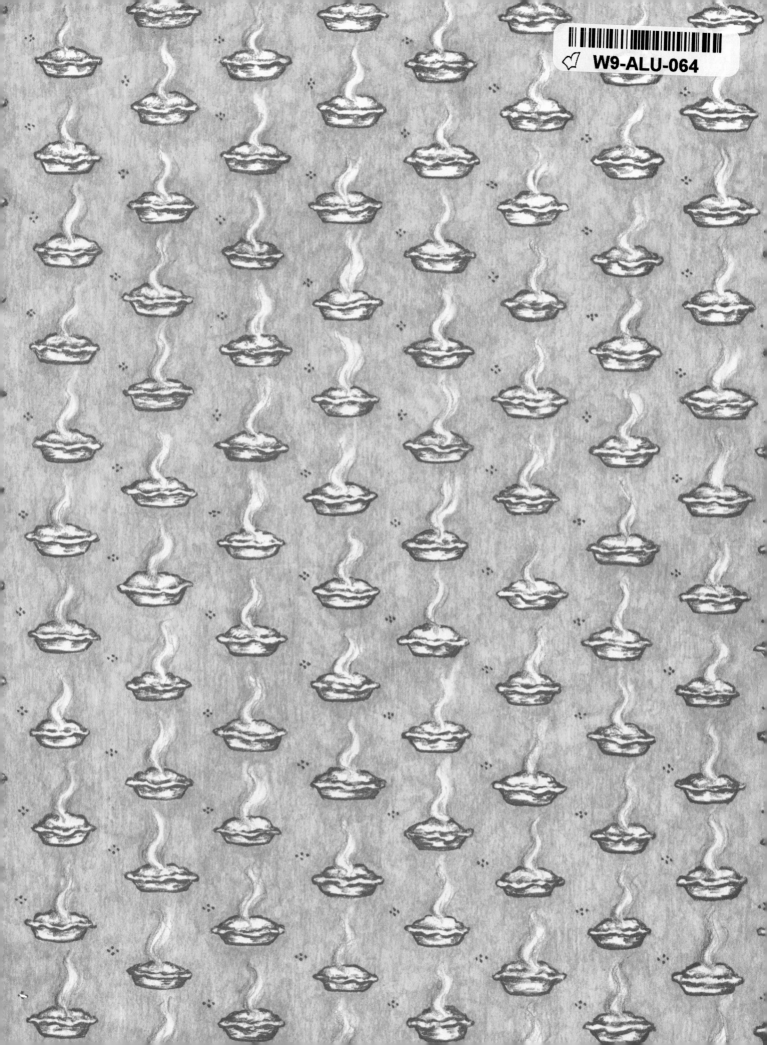

GINA FARINA and the PRINCE of MINTZ

GINA FARINA
and the
PRINCE of MINTZ

Story and Pictures by
Nancy Patz

HARCOURT BRACE JOVANOVICH, PUBLISHERS

San Diego   New York   London

TO
S.L.

Copyright © 1986 by Nancy Patz Blaustein

Library of Congress Cataloging-in-Publication Data
Patz, Nancy.
Gina Farina and the Prince of Mintz.

Summary: The independent Gina Farina, one of a
troupe of traveling players, has a contest of wills
with the grouchy Prince of Mintz when she refuses to
follow his ironclad rules.
[1. Obstinacy—Fiction.   2. Actors and actresses—
Fiction]   I. Title.
PZ7.P27833Gi   1986   [E]   85-16382
ISBN 0-15-230815-6

The drawings in this book were done in pencil on
Strathmore bristol board with three-color separations
by the artist.
The text type was set in Bembo by Thompson Type, San Diego, California.
The display type was hand-lettered by the artist.
Printed by Rae Publishing Co., Inc., Cedar Grove, New Jersey.
Bound by A. Horowitz & Sons, Bookbinders, Fairfield, New Jersey.
Production supervision by Warren Wallerstein.
Designed by Dalia Hartman.

Printed in the United States of America
First edition

A B C D E

Anyone could tell from the map—
Mintz was a strange and dangerous place.
Not even the birds flew free, they say,
and nobody went there except by mistake.
But the story begins in Volzano, long
ago in Volzano.

INA FARINA, the baker's daughter, made marvelous, meaty, *most* unusual, truly splendiferous pies. They were crusty and spicy, with apples and quince—ah, just the slightest *hints* of quince. The people came from miles around to buy them and sing her praises.

But Gina Farina paid no attention.

"That girl has a mind of her own," said the baker, "and her heart's always set on adventure."

It was true. She'd count the weeks until the traveling players came, for they told tales of splendid Ravenna—and Venice where streets were rivers—and Constantinople, city of jewels. Gina Farina would listen for hours.

"To go with the players and travel the world—*that's* what I wish!" she often said.

"What foolishness!" said her father. How could a simple baker's daughter hope to join the famous players?

But Gina Farina had a mind of her own. When the troupe returned to Volzano, she went to the Captain of Players and said,

"The traveling players should have a fine baker. If you'll give me safe passage, sir, I'll bake my pies in return."

Spunky girl, the Captain thought. *And what an elegant treat it would be to eat so well on our journey.* "Come, then, Gina Farina!"

The day soon came for departure.

"Go if you must," said the baker, "but always beware of a town called Mintz. It's ruled by a terrible-tempered prince who punishes all who displease him. *Nobody* ever goes to Mintz—except, my dear, by mistake."

But Gina Farina had a mind of her own, and she paid no attention.

In town after town the players performed, and Gina Farina made specially luscious, deliciously snifforous, truly splendiferous pies.

Then one night when the mist was thick, near Nudelburg, past Boppen-on-Lintz, they found they had wandered

into a strangely grim, gray town.
"What grumpy people!" said Gina Farina.
"This must be Mintz. . . ." said the Captain.
They read the sign on the wall in the square.

RULES OF THE PRINCE OF MINTZ
BEWARE!
Remember by Day. Remember by Night.
IN MINTZ THE PRINCE IS ALWAYS RIGHT!

ALL PERSONS IN THE TOWN OF MINTZ
MUST ACT EXACTLY LIKE THE PRINCE—
AND NO ONE MUST EVER SAY "NO" TO HIM!

Obey these Rules or be locked in the stocks
for a night and a day in the Public Square.
BY ORDER OF THE PRINCE.
BEWARE!

The Captain shuddered. "Bad things happen, I've heard, in Mintz, to people who dare to say 'no' to the Prince."

"Ridiculous!" laughed Gina Farina, and she started her pies for supper.

She baked the crusts. She roasted the meats. She toasted the almonds, candied the sweets, and sprinkled the cinnamon—honeybun cinnamon— over the apples and raisins and quince.

Delicious smells on gentle breezes drifted up . . .

up to the Prince—who sat, as usual, in the top of
the castle turret.

Vincent of Mintz, His Highness the Prince, was a
vain and shamefully grumpy man. He killed a
dragon or two a month and defended his kingdom
now and then, but mostly he sulked in his turret and
thought about nobody but himself.

The people obeyed his Rules, of course, and acted
exactly as he did.

But now His Highness sniffed.

"Spices and meats! Apples and quince! What's
going on down there in Mintz?"

Soon Gina Farina and five hot pies were brought
to the castle by royal command. Vincent devoured
three pies and a half.

"A–humpf," he said, "you must stay and cook in
the castle. You'll bake these pies only for *me*!"

But Gina Farina had a mind of her own. Her
heart was set on adventure.

She looked the Prince in the eye and said,

"No, thank you, Prince!"

"*What* did she say?"

"She said 'no' to the Prince!"

"But nobody ever says 'no' to the Prince!"

"It's never been done before in Mintz!"

"Oh, nobody, nobody—"

"Nobody!"

"*Nobody!*"

"NOBODY ever says 'no' to the Prince!"

Vincent thundered, "*You'll cook in the castle!*"

"Ridiculous!" laughed Gina Farina. "I'm going to see what the world is like! Now if you'll excuse me, sir—" Then Gina Farina went down to the town to finish her pies for supper.

Up in the castle Vincent raged. And since, in Mintz, whatever the *Prince* did, *Mintz* did, people in town did the same.

Vincent stormed, "How *dare* that girl say 'no' to me! She must be punished!"

He called for his Wisest Advisors.

"If she's locked in the stocks in the square," they said, "she cannot bake pies for Your Highness. First give her three chances to change her mind."

"A-humpf!" said the Prince.

The Wisest Advisors continued. "Your Highness himself must *persuade* the maiden, for the pies would be bitter with the baker in chains."

"A-humpf!" grumped His Highness. "Make me a plan."

And so, of course, they did.

"I'll trick her, all right!" vowed Vincent.

Off went the Prince, disguised . . .

as a shepherd from Boppen-on-Lintz.

"Good day, Shepherd!" said Gina Farina. They walked together on the mountain.

"Just one year in seven," the shepherd declared, "the fruit of these trees has a sweetness so rare that people remember it all their days. And this is the year! So surely you'll stay and bake your pies for the fine young Prince."

"Ridiculous!" laughed Gina Farina. "I've a big world to discover!" She looked the shepherd right in the eye. "I think it's a pity about the Prince."

"What's *wrong* with the Prince?" snapped Vincent. Gina Farina just laughed.

"The heart of a grump like that," she said, "will certainly turn to stone. Now don't you agree?" And her laughter echoed on the mountain as she skipped back down to town.

Back in his castle, Vincent was dreadful—sulky
by day, grumpy by night.
  And since, in Mintz, however the *Prince* was,
Mintz was, people in town were the same.

"She has two more chances to change her mind,"
the Wisest Advisors declared. They reached into
their bags of tricks.
  "I'll fool her this time," Vincent muttered.
  And off he went, disguised . . .

as a merchant from Constantinople.

"Good day, Merchant!" said Gina Farina. They walked together in the marketplace.

The merchant declared, "I hear a certain noble Prince will give you pearls and ruby rings and shimmering dresses of dragons' wings if you will stay and bake for him."

"Ridiculous!" laughed Gina Farina. "Who wants dresses of dragons' wings? I want to see what the world is like!" She looked the merchant right in the eye. "It's such a *shame* about the Prince!"

"*Nothing is wrong with Mintz's Prince!*" roared Vincent.

Gina Farina just laughed.

"He's sure to dry up like a prune," she said, "if he sulks all his days in that turret. Now don't you agree?" And her laughter echoed in the marketplace as she danced away.

Life was impossible—truly impossible—up in the castle and down in the town.

"One last chance!" said the Wisest Advisors. They had a special plan.

"She'll never say 'no' to me *now*!" said Vincent.

Off he went, disguised . . .

as a handsome traveling player. *I'm handsome as can be,* he thought. But Gina Farina paid no attention, for this day she was very sad.

The Prince was struck by the sight of her. "Why are you so unhappy?" he asked.

"Our Captain of Players is ill," she said, "and we've no one to take his place. Tonight the people will come for the plays, but there will be no plays to see." Her sigh pierced the heart of the Prince.

I wish I could make her feel better, he thought. But he'd never had such a thought before, and he didn't know what to do.

"I wonder, sir—" said Gina Farina. She looked him right in the eye. "Could *you* help us out?"

"A-humpf!" said Vincent. "Perhaps I can. . . ."

"I know you'll play the part so well!" Gina Farina exclaimed.

And so he did!

Until he got stuck on the dragon's wing.

"A-humpf—*a-humpf!*" he suddenly cried —for as he stumbled, his mask untied and floppingly popped away!

The people gasped.

"The Prince!"

"The Prince!"

"It's really the Prince!"

"That player is really Prince Vincent of Mintz!"

Happy and helpful and not at all grumpy, His Highness was having a *wonderful* time!

Well, *you* know how it is in Mintz. . . .

The people must act just like the Prince!

"Now, really, Your Highness," said Gina Farina,
"won't you get rid of those Rules of Mintz?"

"Not a bad idea!" he said, and he tore down the
sign in the square.

"Not a bad fellow after all!" laughed Gina Farina.

A grand celebration was held in the town for
many a night and many a day.

Then Gina Farina said,

"Now I must go."

"I wish you would stay. I do—" said Vincent.

Gina Farina gently replied, "But I have a very big world to see—and the time has come for the troupe to depart. . . ."

She looked Prince Vincent right in the eye.

"Come *with* us, please do!" she said suddenly.

The Captain of Players said, "We would be honored, Your Highness."

The Prince looked from one to the other.

"Indeed, I'd like to do it—"

"But I am the Prince," he said with pride.
"These are my people, and here I must stay."
"Hurrah!" the people shouted.
The Wisest Advisors smiled.
And so did the baker's daughter.

And then she went on her way—to wondrous adventures in Venice, Ravenna and Constantinople and places she'd never even dreamed of!

But one year in seven, when the fruit of the trees was especially fine, near Nudelburg, past Boppen-on-Lintz . . .

the air would fill with splendiferous smells of
spices and meats and apples and quince—ah, just
the slightest *hints* of quince.

For the traveling players would return. . . .

Then Gina Farina would laugh again with the Prince of Mintz.

And the sound of their laughter had a sweetness so rare that people remembered it all their days.

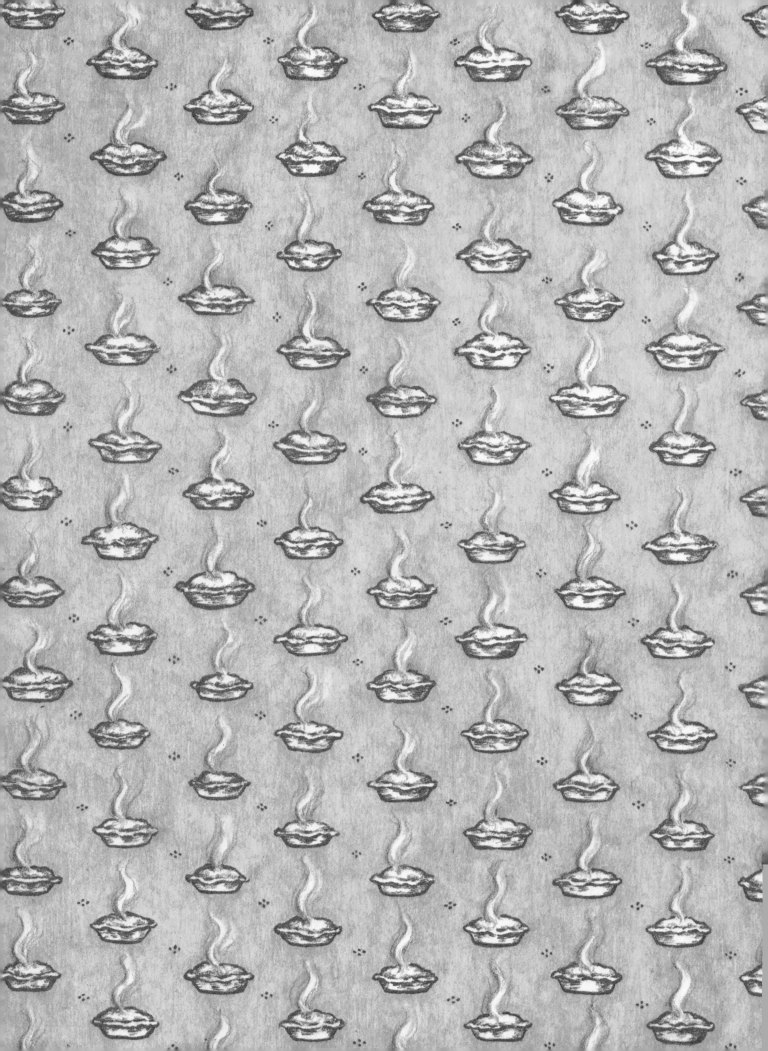